The Animal Show

by Liza Charlesworth

ISBN: 978-1-338-78268-4
Illustrated by Chester Bentley
Copyright © 2021 by Liza Charlesworth. All rights reserved.
Published by Scholastic Inc., 557 Broadway, New York, NY 10012

10 9 8 7 6 5 4 3 2 1   68   21 22 23 24 25 26 27/0

Printed in Jiaxing, China. First printing, June 2021.

One bear stands
on top of the elephant.
Oh, my!

Then **one** pig stands
on top of the bear.
Oh, my!

Then **one** fox stands
on top of the pig.
Oh, my!

Then **one** dog stands
on top of the fox.
Oh, my!

Then **one** bunny stands
on top of the dog.
Oh, my!

Then the **one** bunny sneezes.

Oh, my!